MR. SNIFFLES'

THIS BOOK BELONGS TO:

Written by Shelly Mack

Illustrated by Jose Jr. Dakay

Editor: Stephanie R. Graham
Editor: Kirsten Rees | MakeMeASuccess
Cover Designer: Jose Jr. Dakay
Illustrator: Jose Jr. Dakay

This book is dedicated to my mum and dad.
Thank you for giving me a place in this world.
Love you always. xx

♡ shelly :)

Acknowledgements

I would like to thank Frazer Nangle, Jose Jr. Dakay, Stephanie R. Graham, Kirsten Rees, Manuel Quintana, Jacqueline Nangle, Colin Mackenzie, Cindy Mackenzie, Bruce Mackenzie, Louise Grant, and Scott Grant.

Mr. Sniffles is a germ,
the round, squidgy kind.
He grabs and he sticks
on to anything he can find.

He's invisible to humans,
yet so easy to catch.
It's truly amazing
how he can attach.

Tiny feelers on his head
stand and point out.
And his big, sucking lips
stick when he pouts.

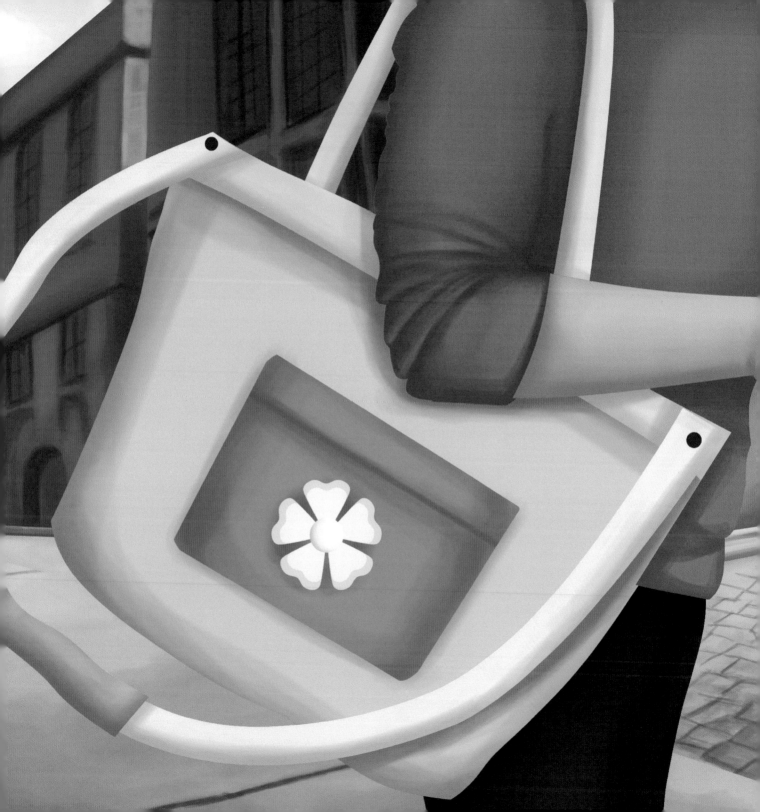

He's blown from noses
and coughed up with wheezes,
passed from hand to hand
and *ah-chooed* with sneezes.

ACHOO

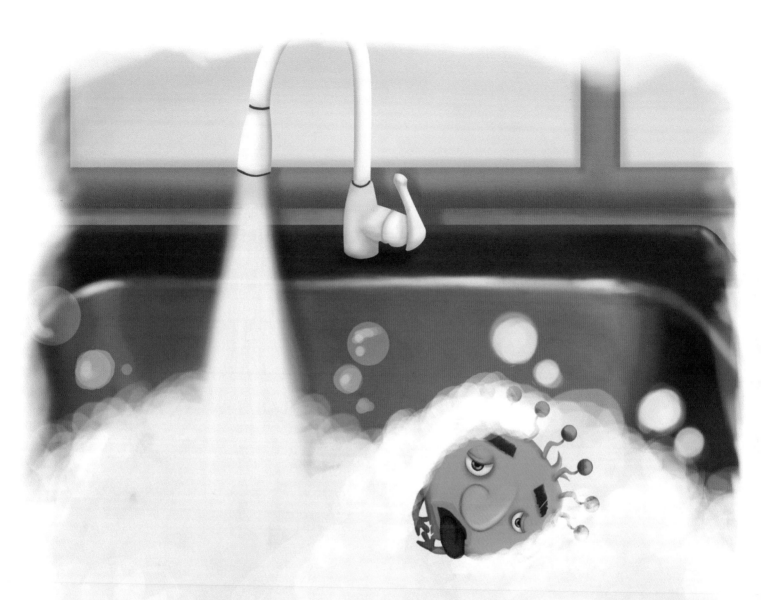

**What he hates the most,
as it makes him choke,
is being put into water
and covered in soap.**

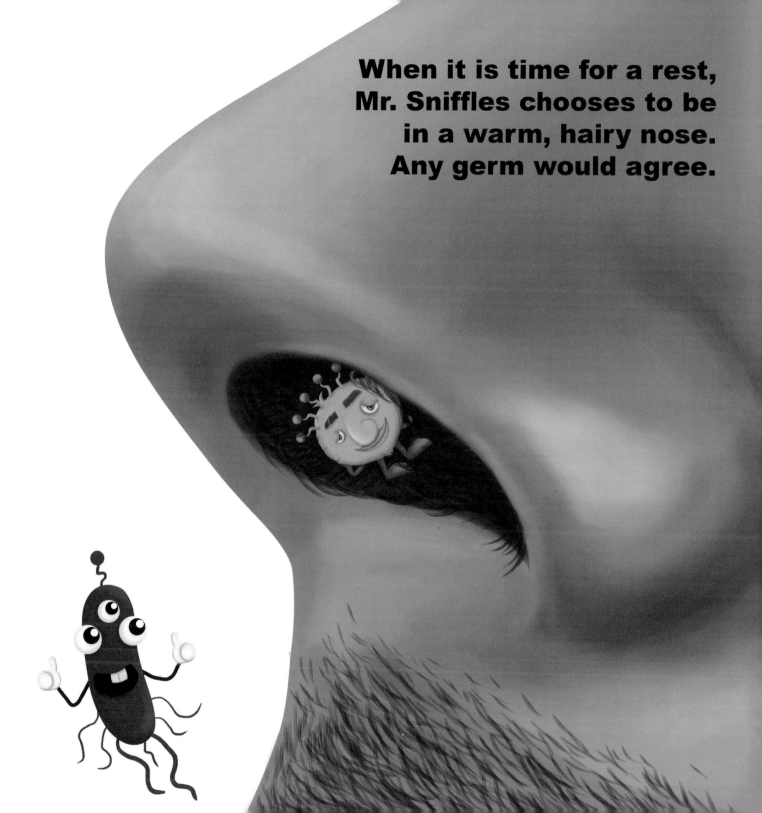

When it is time for a rest,
Mr. Sniffles chooses to be
in a warm, hairy nose.
Any germ would agree.

He closes his eyes.
Morning will come soon.

Hello to the sun.
Goodbye to the moon.

Every day, he seeks adventure in all different places.

He goes from pillar to post, from hands to faces.

He jumps over houses
and slides down the stairs,

**rolls through cupboards
and whizzes over chairs.**

Mr. Sniffles goes everywhere.
He travels afar,
on planes and trains.
He even rides in cars.

He sees beautiful places,
like Paris and Japan.

Today, he is shopping in a place called Milan.

Each day is exciting, having a new place to go.

He enjoys the cinema and theatre shows.

He waves to fellow germs each day on the go.

HELLO!!

They always wave back and shout out, "Hello!"

Mr. Sniffles wants to stop, but he doesn't have long before a person or tissue makes him long gone.

As he gets older,
it gets hard on his own.
He starts to realise
he's sad being alone.

One day, he detaches
and jumps to the floor.
He is in a big house
he's never been in before.

He rolls and explores
until he starts to tire.
Then, he takes a rest
beside a nice, warm fire.

That's when he hears the voices all around. He moves very slowly, not making a sound.

The voices all stop
as his eyes sweep the ground.
All kinds of germs
he has suddenly found!

NEW GERM!

They all look at Mr. Sniffles
with shock and surprise.
Then, they call him over
with their sweet little cries.

"A new germ! A new germ!
Come on, join our crew.
We are a family,
and we welcome you!"

"There are thousands of us here,
if you want to stay.
You can make this your home
to come back to each day."

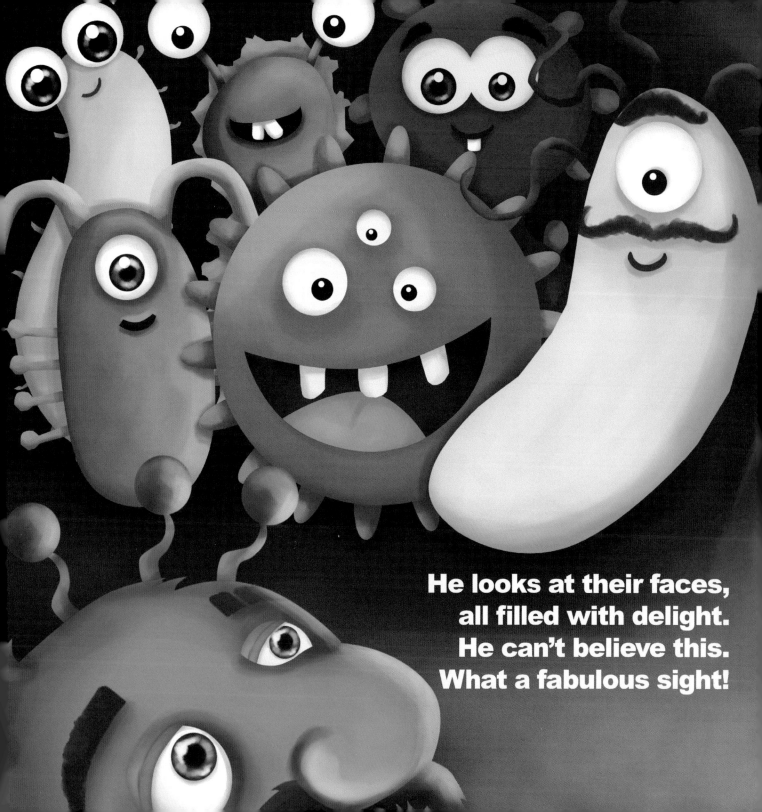

He looks at their faces,
all filled with delight.
He can't believe this.
What a fabulous sight!

A new home and a family,
a place he can stay.
This really has been
the most marvellous day!

They invite him over
to their big family rug.
Never has a bug
ever felt so snug.

If you would like to read more Shelly Mack stories, leave a little encouragement here:
Amazon
Goodreads
Facebook

Connect with Shelly Mack on social media and visit her website to
sign up on the mailing list for book updates and competitions:

Website: www.shellymackbooks.com
Instagram: @shellymackbooks
Twitter: @Shellymackbooks
Facebook: Shellymackbooks
Email: shellymackbooks@gmail.com

Books by Shelly Mack:

Go-Go the Gallimimus (Coming Soon)

The Animal Series:

The Turtle and the Spider: A Very Sweet Adventure
Spikey the Hedgehog: The Big Accident (Coming Soon)

Germ Awareness Series:

Mr. Sniffles (Book 1)
Dot the Snot (Book 2 – Coming Soon)

Shellymackbooks

Printed in Poland
by Amazon Fulfillment
Poland Sp. z o.o., Wrocław